SILLY SYDNEY
by TONY GARTH

Sydney was a very silly boy.

From the moment he woke up to the moment he went to bed, Sydney was silly.

One morning, Sydney got up and began to get dressed.

He put his socks on his hands, his pants on his head, a wellington boot on one foot and a flipper on the other.

"You can't go to school dressed like that!" his Mum said. "Go and get changed at once!"

But Sydney's silliness didn't stop there. At breakfast, he poured orange juice on his cereal, drank his milk from an egg cup and buttered his toast the wrong side up.

Worse was to come. The first lesson at school was art. Sydney liked art. Except that he painted himself instead of the paper.

When it came to games, Sydney wasn't picked for any of the school teams. No one could tell what he wanted to play.

It was time for lunch. Sydney's friends crowded round to see what he had in his lunch box.

Would it be hot dogs with chocolate sauce?

Or sardine and marshmallow sandwiches?

Or a frothy milk shake made with tomatoes?

But when Sydney took off the lid, all they could see was one banana and two slices of bread.

"That's not silly at all," they groaned. But Sydney didn't let them down. He put a slice of bread behind each ear, and began to munch the banana skin, instead of the banana.

The next day was Sydney's birthday. His parents had promised to take him and his sister to 'Adventure World' as a special treat.

Sydney's parents had a word of warning.

"Now, Sydney," they said. "Try to behave. Don't wander off and DON'T be silly..."

But of course, he was.

There was lots to do in 'Adventure World' - a haunted house, a candy-floss stall, a roller coaster and, best of all, a zoo full of wild animals, including a gigantic gorilla.

It was a long time since breakfast and Sydney was hungry. He went to buy a hot dog. He bought one for his sister and one for himself. Except that Sydney's hot dog didn't have onions, or mustard, or bread. It didn't even have a hot dog - just a great dollop of tomato ketchup.

All of a sudden, there was a terrible commotion. People began screaming and running this way and that.

"The gorilla's escaped," somebody shouted. "Run for your life!"

Sydney turned to grab his sister's hand...

...but it was too late. She was gone.

She had wandered off, right into the path of the gigantic gorilla.

"Don't worry! I'm on my way!" shouted Sydney and ran to her rescue.

"Oh no!" cried Sydney's parents. "He's bound to do something silly now."

And sure enough...he did!

Sydney pulled some silly faces and made lots of silly noises. Then he did some of his best silly walks and was generally as silly as he could possibly be.

The gorilla was so confused he completely forgot why he'd escaped and let his keeper lead him away.

How everyone cheered! Silly Sydney had saved his sister. What a hero!

The owner of 'Adventure World' presented Sydney with a shiny medal and a free pass for life.

"That was a very sensible thing to do, young Sydney," he said. "In a silly sort of way."

On the way home, a thought struck Sydney.

"I've never been sensible in my life before," he said.
"Perhaps I should try it more often!"

Sydney's parents were very glad to hear it.

"I'll start tomorrow," Sydney said. And pulled a
very silly face at the lady in the car behind.

Look out for the next twelve Little Monsters!

FRIENDLY FRANCO

CLUMSY CLARISSA

BOISTEROUS BILLY

SICKLY SIMON

SERIOUS SADIE

GROWN-UP GABBY

PERFECT PRUDENCE

RUDE ROGER

DANGEROUS DAVE

CURIOUS CALVIN

DIRTY DERMOT

TANTRUM TABITHA